Justin Potemkin
and the
500-Mile Race

Justin Potemkin
and the 500-Mile Race

Written and Illustrated by
Peter J. Welling

PELICAN PUBLISHING COMPANY
Gretna 2004

To the memory of Tony Bettenhausen, Shirley (nee McElreath) Bettenhausen, Russ Roberts and Larry Rangel, who finished the race together, and to all those who pursue the checkered flag

Thanks to the driver of the Dar-Car.
Thanks to Lisa P. Christian, Dina, and her teacher,
Kristy Von Ogden, for the Russian translations. Spocibo.

The word "Pelican" and the depiction of a pelican are trademarks of Pelican Publishing Company, Inc., and are registered in the U.S. Patent and Trademark Office.

Library of Congress Cataloging-in-Publication Data

Welling, Peter J.
    Justin Potemkin and the 500-mile race / written and illustrated by Peter J. Welling.
        p. cm.
Summary: After losing the Russian 500 Mile Race to the deceitful Czar Mos, Justin the rabbit and his friends move to America and plan a rematch automobile race at Indianapolis.
    ISBN 1-58980-149-0 (hardcover : alk. paper)
    [1. Automobile racing—Fiction. 2. Rabbits--Fiction. 3. Animals—Fiction.] I. Title: Justin Potemkin and the five hundred-mile race. II. Title.
    PZ7 .W4573 Ju 2004
    [E] —dc22

                                                    2003018913

Printed in China

Published by Pelican Publishing Company, Inc.
1000 Burmaster Street, Gretna, Louisiana 70053

JUSTIN POTEMKIN AND THE 500-MILE RACE

The story of Justin Potemkin and the 500-Mile Race began long ago in Russia, sort of. Each May, Czar Mos Romoonoff sponsored the Russian 500-Mile Race. He always drove in it and always won, too, usually by cheating.

"This year's winner gets a town named after him and a gallon of Royal Russian milk, too," Mos said.

"Who needs it?" Justin mumbled.

"What's wrong, Justin Pumpkin? Got milk?" Lenin Tortoise asked.

"The name is *Potemkin*," Justin said.

"No one cares, loser," Lenin said.

Ever since Justin's Grandpa Rufus lost the famous Tortoise-Hare Race to Lenin's Grandpa Norton years ago, no hare anywhere had won anything. Justin didn't care about the prize. He just wanted to win.

"Are you ready to race?" Justin's mechanic, Bob Potamus, asked.

"I was born ready," Justin replied. He said hello to the American, Flamingo Joe, and to the Australian, Phil Didgeridoo. Then Justin greeted Czar Mos. "Your highness, I'm Justin Potemkin."

"Did you say *Pumpkin*?" Mos asked.

"No, no, *Potemkin*," Justin said.

"Aren't you a peasant?" the czar asked.

"Yes," Justin stammered.

"Then no one cares what your name is," Mos laughed. He jammed a bullhorn on Justin's head. "Goodbye bunny!" he shouted.

The drivers stampeded to their cars.

"Let's mooove out," Mos bellowed into the bullhorn.

"How far are we racing this time?" Lenin Tortoise asked.

"Five hundred miles or until I win," Czar Mos said with a wink.

"Did you hear that, Bob?" Justin asked.

"Sure," Bob said, "the czar always wins."

"But I can still beat the tortoise, right?" Justin asked.

"I doubt it," Bob said. The czar's mother, Margaret Moo, dropped her green shawl to start the race.

And Mos started cheating. He threw tacks on the track.
The German car blew a tire and crashed on a golf course.
"Ach du lieber, look at my tires! There is a hole in one,"
Garret von Garret the German shrieked.

"I'm toast," Jacque Jambon whined, after Mos jammed the French car. Mos then shoved the Chinese car into a swimming pool.

"Hsing-hsing, ling-ling, and Beijing, too," Panda Ming yelled. "You mad cow! I am so angry I could chop sticks!"

Mos flipped the Australian car upside down. Phil Didgeridoo was hopping mad.

"That bloke is nastier than a bald bunyip," he said. Mos pushed another Russian, Ivan Vod, into the river.

"What a twist," Ivan cried as the Vod car sank.

Czar Mos spotted Justin heading for the hills. "Here I come, Justin Pumpkin," he yelled.

"The name is *Potemkin*!" Justin shouted. Justin's tire struck a rock. Down the mountain went the rolling stone, but it gathered no Mos.

Justin drove from the mountains to the valleys. He drove over the river and through the woods to grandmother's house. He waved to his cousin Peter as he passed Mr. McGregor's place. Right on his bunny tail was Czar Mos.

The next thing Justin knew, he was coming round the mountain again and leaving Russia behind. They passed the "Welcome to Finland" sign at the Finnish border. Then the one thing that no one expected to happen happened.

They ran out of gas. Every car sputtered to a stop in front of Voitto's Diner. Voitto came out, waved his checkered tablecloth, and set the table.

"Come, eat and drink," he said.

"But, who won the race?" Justin asked.

"I did, of course," Czar Mos said. "So I shall build a town and call it Mos Cow, after me. And it is a good thing I won, too. Who would want to live in a town called Pumpkin?"

"*Potemkin*," Justin groaned. "Who came in second?"
"Hmmm," Czar Mos said. "I'll pick . . . Lenin."
"Thank you," Lenin said. "I certainly deserve it."
"And who gets the bill for dinner?" Voitto asked.
"I'll pick *him*," Mos said and pointed at Justin.

"That is *so* unfair," Justin said.

"Yes, it is," Flamingo Joe said. "Why don't you and Bob come to America and pursue your dream there?"

"We will," Justin said. "Um, can you get the tip? I'm a little short."

Justin and Bob joined Flamingo Joe in Indianapolis. They built a brick racetrack and won many races, but something was missing.

"I want to beat that tortoise," Justin said, "and Czar Mos, too."

"Then let's do it," Flamingo Joe said.

Thirty-three drivers were invited to be in the first 500-mile Memorial Day Race in Indianapolis. The first to arrive was Lenin Tortoise, with his new Red Star car. Mos brought the Czar car, but it was getting old and rusty.

"Whether your car is old or new, Justin Potemkin is going to beat you," Bob said.

"Did he say Justin Pumpkin?" Lenin whispered.

"Got me," Mos said. Bob uncovered Justin's red, white, and blue racecar. "Behold 'the American Dream,'" he said.

The next day, they lined up.

"No cheating," Justin said.

"No beef here," Mos said. "There's too much at stake."

"My car is souped up," Lenin said. "I'll leave you in the dust, bunny. Let the race begin."

Mos cut off the hare, but Justin braked. Lenin swerved and rammed the Czar car. The Czar car crashed, and Mos landed in a milk truck in the infield.

"Careful," Lenin shouted, "the milk's deep. It's past your eyes."

Justin won the race easily. The hare stood up on the back of the wrecked Czar car.
"Rabbits rule!" he shouted.

"You were lucky, Justin Pumpkin," Lenin snapped.
"*Potemkin*," Justin said. "And, of course, I'm lucky. I have *two* rabbit's feet."
"Milk anyone?" Mos asked.

Years have passed, but the greatest spectacle in racing is still held in Indianapolis in May. The brick racetrack is now called the Indianapolis Motor Speedway. Instead of Margaret Moo's cape, the race starts with the waving of a green flag.

A checkered flag replaced Voitto's tablecloth, but drivers are still "Russian" toward the "Finnish" line. The winner always gets a glass of milk. Many say it is because of Mos. Indiana cows disagree. "We don't mean to split hares, but that is udder nonsense," they moo.

Years later, the three friends bought a farm. Bob sells flavored milk at a roadside stand. Flamingo Joe sells lawn decorations, of himself. And the bunny with the fastest tractor in the state raises—yup, you guessed it—Justin's pumpkins.

Cheese	Sihr	(seeyr)
Oh, dear me	Ach du lieber	(German)
Thank you	Spocibo	(spah cee bah)
Welcome	Dobra poshalovat	(da brO pazha lavat)

Konetc (ken yetz)
The End

GLOSSARY

Page	Animal Name/	in Russian	Pronunciation	Animal Sound in Russian
5	Cow	Karova	(ka-rO-vah)	Muu
6	Duck	Utka	(oot-kah)	Krya-krya
7	Cuckoo	Kukushk	(koo-kosh-kah)	Ku-ku
8	Goose	Gus	(goos)	Ga-ga
9	Rooster	Petukh	(pee-toohuh)	Ku-ka-re-ku
10	Crow	Varona	(va-rO-nah)	Kar-kar
11	Bee	Pchela	(p-chill-ah)	Zh-zh-zh
12	Mice	Mysh'	(myeesh)	Pee-pee-pee
13	Frog	Lyagushka	(lee-goosh-kah)	Kva-kva
14	Bird	Ptichka	(p-teach-kah)	Chik-chirik
15	Owl	Sova	(sah-vah')	Uh-uh-uh
16	Dog	Sobaka	(sa-ba-kah)	Gav-gav
17	Pig	Svin'ya	(sveen-yah)	Khryu-khyru
18	Donkey	Osel	(ah-syole)	Ia-ia
19	Chicken	Kuritsa	(koo'ree-sta)	Ko-ko-ko
20	Cat	Koshka	(kosh-kah)	Myau
21	Chicks	Tsypylyata	(tsee-plee-ya-tah)	Chee-chee-chee
22	Rabbit	Zayatc	(za yitz)	—
22	Hippopotamus	Gippopatam	(geepa pah tom)	—
23	Beaver	Babir	(babyoor)	—
24	Goat	Koza	(ka-zah)	Mee
25	Horse	Loshad	(low-shIdes)	I-go-go
26	Tiger	Tigr	(tce-grr)	R-r-r-r
27	Sheep	Ovsta	(off-sta)	Bee
28	Dove	Golub	(gO-lub)	Kurr-kurr
29	Puppy	Shchenok	(shinock)	Tyav-tyav